MAGGIE PEARSON

SHORT AND SHOCKING!

A book of very short shocking stories

OXFORD
UNIVERSITY PRESS

OXFORD
UNIVERSITY PRESS

Great Clarendon Street, Oxford OX2 6DP

Oxford University Press is a department of the University of Oxford.
It furthers the University's objective of excellence in research, scholarship,
and education by publishing worldwide in

Oxford   New York

Auckland   Cape Town   Dar es Salaam   Hong Kong   Karachi
Kuala Lumpur   Madrid   Melbourne   Mexico City   Nairobi
New Delhi   Shanghai   Taipei   Toronto

With offices in

Argentina   Austria   Brazil   Chile   Czech Republic   France   Greece
Guatemala   Hungary   Italy   Japan   Poland   Portugal   Singapore
South Korea   Switzerland   Thailand   Turkey   Ukraine   Vietnam

Oxford is a registered trade mark of Oxford University Press
in the UK and in certain other countries

British Library Cataloguing in Publication Data available

ISBN 978-0-19-278191-8

11

Printed in Great Britain

Illustrated by Chris Mould

Paper used in the production of this book is a natural,
recyclable product made from wood grown in sustainable forestgs.
The manufacturing process conforms to the environmental
regulations of the country of origin.

Contents

Whoo-oo!

An old woman sat by the fire alone. And she was sick of it.

Night after night her old man went toddling off to the pub and never came back till past closing time.

'I'll teach him!' she muttered. 'I'll frighten him so he'll never go out after dark again.'

She took an old sheet and she cut two eye-holes in it. Then she flung it over her head and hurried down to the church porch and waited for her old man to come wandering by on his way home. Out she popped, wearing that old sheet, waving her arms about and crying, 'Whoo-oo! Whoo-oo!'

The old man stopped. He turned to look at her. He smiled. 'Is it you again, you old ghost?' he said. 'And tonight you've brought a friend along to keep you company. That's nice.'

Behind her the old woman heard a voice whispering: 'Whoo-oo! Whoo-oo!'

The Road to Samarra

A merchant of Baghdad was sipping sherbet in his garden one day when one of his servants came running towards him and flung himself down at his feet.

'Master!' he cried. 'Save me! I have just seen Death walking in your garden. She looked straight at me. I was sure she had come for me. Master, I beg you, lend me a horse so I can ride far away, to a place where Death will not find me!'

'Take the swiftest horse in my stable,' said the merchant. 'But where will you go?'

'I have a cousin who lives in Samarra. I can be there by nightfall.'

'Then go now,' said the merchant. 'With my blessing.'

Off rode the servant, with the wind at his heels.

The merchant went walking through his garden until he saw Death still standing where his servant had left her. The merchant was a wise man, not afraid to meet Death face to face.

'Why did you threaten my servant just now?' he asked her.

Death shook her head and smiled. 'Did I frighten

him? I didn't mean to. I was just so astonished to see him here in Baghdad, because I am supposed to meet him come nightfall in Samarra.'

The Boggart

If you don't know what a boggart is, thank your lucky stars. A boggart is a poltergeist with attitude. Bumps in the night is just for starters.

There was a poor farmer and his wife who were plagued by a boggart. It curdled the milk and juggled the new-laid eggs till they smashed themselves on the floor. It used to swing on the washing-line till it broke and the clothes all fell down in the mud. Then it would tramp all round the house leaving big muddy footprints. Just when they'd settled themselves for a nice quiet evening by the fire, that boggart would start huffing and puffing down the chimney, sending smoke and soot every which way.

Sometimes things would go quiet for a bit—maybe for days at a time—and they might start hoping it had gone for good. Then at three in the morning they'd be woken by the boggart singing to itself in a deep bass voice that turned their insides to a jelly.

When it took to rocking the baby's cradle so hard the poor little mite kept falling out onto the floor, 'That's it!' said the farmer's wife. 'Either that boggart goes or I do!'

'We'll all go,' whispered the farmer.

They waited till the boggart had one of its quiet days. Then they loaded up the cart with as much as it would carry.

They listened till they could hear the boggart singing on the other side of the house.

The wife left her knitting on the kitchen table because the chance to unravel it was something the boggart never could resist.

Then they climbed on the cart and set off.

Halfway down the lane they met a neighbour. He knew all about the boggart. He looked at the load on the cart and said, 'You've had enough, then?'

'We have!' said the farmer.

'So you're flitting?'

Before the farmer could answer, a voice that turned their insides to a jelly came from deep down among the baggage on the cart: 'Aye!' it rumbled cheerfully. 'We're flitting.'

The Two Husbands

'Men!' said Molly. 'They are so-o-oo stupid!'
'Tell me about it!' said Polly. 'My husband will believe anything I tell him.'
'He can't be stupider than mine.'
'Oh no?'

When Molly got home to her husband, 'Happy birthday!' she said.

'Is it my birthday?' He opened the box she gave him. It looked empty.

'Don't you like the new suit I bought you?' she said. 'Let me help you on with it. There you go! Light as a feather, isn't it?'

'Very nice, very smart,' says he, strutting round the house in his underwear.

Meanwhile Polly goes home, takes one look at her husband and, 'You should be in bed!' she says.

'Should I?' says he.

'You're ill. Maybe even dying.'

Next morning: 'Just as I feared! You're dead,' says she.

'Am I?' says he. 'I suppose you're right.' And lies

12

down in the coffin, good as gold, while she phones up all their friends and relations to come to the wake. First outing for Molly's husband's fine, new invisible suit.

All the friends and relations, well, they know it's supposed to be a sad occasion, but—walking round in his underwear, you've got to laugh, haven't you? Laugh they did, till their sides were aching and the tears were running down their cheeks.

Till a voice came from the coffin: 'I'd be laughing too, if I wasn't dead!'

Old Ted (1)

Early one morning I met old Ted coming up the lane on his way to work. Eyes half shut and dragging his feet, like he hadn't slept.

'What's up?' I asked him. 'You look like you haven't slept.'

'No more I have,' said he. 'I was waiting up till dawn for my cat to come in, so I could put him out for the night.'

Old Ted (2)

Old Ted said: 'Did you hear the one about the Irishman who was sentenced to death?

'They told him, "You can make one statement before you die. If you tell us the truth, we'll shoot you. If you lie, we'll hang you."

'"Here's my statement, then," said the Irishman. "I shall be hanged."

'Think about it,' said Old Ted as he went out the pub door.

I'm still thinking.

The Two Pickpockets

Jimmy the Dip was the King of Pickpockets. No contenders. Till his own pocket was picked by Light-fingered Lil while he was busy picking hers.

In that moment they knew they were made for each other.

So they were married and they had a baby. Such plans they had! What a pickpocket he was going to be! The greatest pickpocket that ever was.

But when the baby was born, poor mite—'Look at his little arm,' sighed Lil. Jimmy nodded sadly. 'He'll never make a pickpocket.'

The baby's right fist was clenched like a bird's claw, tight up against his little chest. When Jimmy tried to straighten its arm, the baby yelled blue murder.

Every time someone touched that arm, the baby yelled. The doctor did his best, but the baby roared still louder.

'Get me a specialist!' said Jimmy.

The specialist came, from Harley Street, in his big, black, shiny Rolls Royce car.

The baby looked at him as if to say, 'Touch me and I'll scream!'

The great man knew better than to try. He held up his pretty gold watch for the baby to see.

16

Backwards and forwards the baby's eyes followed the gold watch swinging on its golden chain as the specialist bent to examine him.

Then its little right arm shot out, its fist unclenched and something rattled to the floor as it grabbed the watch and held it tight.

Jimmy the Dip bent down and picked up the thing the child had dropped. It was the midwife's wedding-ring. The little fellow had been hanging on to it from the first moment he was born.

'There!' says Jimmy. 'Didn't I say he was going to grow up to be the greatest pickpocket that ever was?'

And, sad to say, he did.

The Old Woman and Death

An old gypsy woman went collecting sticks for the fire.

She was old—so old! Her feet hurt and her bones ached. Her eyesight was going and her teeth had mostly gone and the wood she'd gathered would barely keep her warm for another day.

'Come, Death!' she whispered wearily. 'Where are you when a body needs you?'

'Here,' said Death, 'right by your side. What can I do for you, old woman?'

'Ah! If you can just help me lift that bundle of sticks on my back so I can carry it home, then I'll be right as ninepence!'

The Tinker and the Huntsman

A tinker sat under a hedge, mending a saucepan—tap, tap, tap! with his hammer—when a rabbit came running past.

There goes my supper! thought the tinker as he threw his hammer after it—just as a huntsman fired his gun.

The rabbit fell dead.

'Mine, I think,' said the huntsman.

'Mine!' said the tinker.

'Let's go back to my place,' said the huntsman. 'We can talk it over there.'

So back they went. The huntsman's wife had supper ready on the table. A very good supper it was.

The huntsman said: 'It's too late now to decide who owns that rabbit. Let's talk it over in the morning. Sweet dreams!'

'We should both have sweet dreams,' said the tinker, 'after that meal your wife cooked for us. I tell you what! Whichever of us has the sweetest dream shall keep the rabbit.'

'Done!' said the huntsman.

He and his wife went up to bed while the tinker curled up in his cloak beside the kitchen fire.

*　　*　　*

Next morning when the huntsman and his wife came downstairs, 'Did you have sweet dreams?' he asked the tinker.

'The sweetest!'

'Not half as sweet as mine, I'm sure! I dreamed of a ladder leading right up to heaven, where there were flowers everywhere, and fountains of sweet water and the most beautiful music playing. I didn't want to wake up. Now where's that rabbit?'

'Well, there's a strange thing!' said the tinker. 'I dreamed very much the same dream myself. I watched you climb that ladder up to heaven and I could see how happy you were with all the fountains and the flowers and the music. I didn't think you'd ever be coming back. So—waste not, want not!—I ate the rabbit for my breakfast. And very good it was, too!'

The King of the Jungle

'Who's the King of the Jungle?' Lion roared.

'You are, Lion!' cried the zebras, trying hard to make themselves invisible among the tall grasses.

Lion tossed his golden mane. 'Who's the King of the Jungle?'

'You are, your highness!' The giraffes bowed their long necks down to the ground.

Lion bared his sharp white teeth. 'Who's the King of the Jungle?'

'You are!' chattered the monkeys, taking to the trees. 'No question!'

Lion swished his tail and stalked on. 'Who's the King of the Jungle?' he roared.

'You are, your majesty!' the gazelles agreed.

'Your excellency!' murmured the smaller animals lurking in the shadows.

'Your wonderfulness!' echoed the smallest of all, terrified of being stepped on.

Lion met an elephant standing in the middle of the path.

'Who's the King of the Jungle?' Lion roared.

The elephant reached out his trunk, picked up Lion

by the tail, whirled him three times round his head and tossed him into a thornbush; hooked him out, dragged him down to the river and threw him in.

Bruised and bleeding, dizzy and dripping wet, Lion crawled out. 'No need to lose your temper,' he growled, 'just because you don't know the answer.'

Three Foolish Fishermen

In a little boat bobbing on a blue-green sea three fishermen sat, fishing. They'd fished all day and caught nothing.

The sun went down and the stars came out. Still they sat. Still nothing. Then suddenly—'What's that?'

'What's what?'

'Down there! Deep down in the water. It looks like—'

'Looks like—'

'Gold!' A shimmering disc of pure gold.

'Why, it's as big as a dinner plate!'

'Bigger! There must be enough gold there to make us all rich for life!'

'Hold hard! I saw it first.' Without more ado, the first fisherman dived in. Two minutes later he bobbed up again.

'Did you find it?'

'Where is it, then?'

'I couldn't stay down long enough. I need something to weigh me down.'

So back to the shore they rowed, lickety-spit, to fill their pockets up with stones. Then put to sea again, till they reached the place where they could see that disc of brightest gold shining through the water.

The first fisherman dived in again, the stones in his pockets this time carrying him straight to the bottom. Five minutes the other two waited. Ten.

Said one to the other, 'He must have found it by now.'

Said the other to the one, 'Could be it's too heavy to lift. I'll go and help him.' In he dived, the stones in his pockets taking him down.

Five minutes the third man waited. Ten. Fifteen! I know what's going on! he thought; they're going to sneak off with that gold between them, and I'll be left with nothing!

So in he dived, after them, down, down, down. Leaving the little boat bobbing alone on the sea.

And the full moon shining above, gazing down at her yellow-gold reflection in the water.

A Handful of Dust

I never saw so many old bottles as there were in that antique shop; bottles of all shapes, sizes, and colours. And one that stood alone on a corner shelf.

'She's not for sale,' the man said.

'She?'

'I call her Sybil.'

'Do all your bottles have names?'

'Not the bottle; what's in the bottle.'

I picked it up so I could see more clearly.

'Don't shake it about! She doesn't like it.'

'Sybil?'

'That's right.'

It was just a little heap of dust. The bottle was old—very old.

'That's Roman, that is,' said the man.

'As old as that! And Sybil?'

'She's Roman, too. The way I was told it, she used to be some kind of priestess—and good at her job, too. So good, the god himself came down and offered to grant her just one wish.'

'What did she wish for?'

'Eternal life, of course! There was just one snag—'

'There always is!'

'She still went on growing old. Her flesh withered and her teeth and hair fell out and everyone she knew and cared about was long, long dead. She shrank till she was nothing but skin and bone—but she was still alive! And the skin and bone crumbled to the handful of dust which you see there, in that bottle.'

'And still alive?'

He nodded.

'That's a good story,' I said. 'You sure you don't want to sell it?'

He shook his head.

I set the bottle down gently and turned to go. From behind me I heard a voice, softer than the wind rustling through dry grass: 'I wish to die!'

The Fallen Angel Cake

I'm not saying my mum's a bad cook. But the angel cake she baked for the cake stall at the village fête was a disaster. It looked like the cat had sat on it.

'If I turn it upside down,' she said, 'and ice it—the dent in the middle won't show.'

She turned it upside down—and the middle fell out.

'Don't cry,' I said. 'We can fill up the hole with something round and not too heavy—'

'Like what?' she said.

'Like a toilet roll! Cover the lot over with icing. And I'll nip down to the fête as soon as it opens and buy it back!'

So that's what we did.

Except I couldn't buy it back. Mum's cake wasn't on the cake stall.

We spent the whole afternoon trying to find out what had happened to it. We were still there when it came to the clearing up. So we helped with that. Then Chloe's mum invited us all back to her place.

I knew how it would be: tea in bone china cups, funny little forks to eat the cake with and having to take our shoes off so as not to mark the carpet.

It was worse than that. Much worse.

Right in the middle of the table sat my mum's cake!

We were getting up the courage to confess when someone said: 'Oh! What a beautiful cake!'

Chloe's mum beamed. 'Thank you,' she said. 'I baked it myself.'

Old Ted (3)

'GM foods!' said Old Ted. 'Genetic engineering! That's nothing new. When I was nobut a nipper, my old dad bred a six-legged chicken.'

'Why would he do that, Old Ted?'

'There were six of us in the family, see? Mum, Dad, and four kids. He got sick of us arguing every time we had chicken for dinner, over whose turn it was to have a leg.'

'What did it taste like, then?'

'I don't know. We never could catch the darn thing to find out!'

Old Ted (4)

Late one night, I came upon Old Ted crawling round and round a lamp-post.

'I'm not drunk,' he said. 'I'm looking for my keys. Reckon I dropped them as I was coming out of the village hall.'

'Why are you looking for them here, then?'

'Reckon I stand more chance of finding them where the light's better.'

The Magic Canoe

In the rain forest . . .

A man carved himself a canoe out of an old hollow tree.

He didn't know there was a spirit living in that tree.

Next day, when he came to go fishing, he heard *swish-swish!* through the bushes, and the *flip-flop!* of two little feet. He saw his canoe walking towards him, wearing a great big smile on the face he'd painted on its prow.

So in he climbed and off they went—*flip-flop*, along the forest path; *swish-swish* through the bushes—till they came to the river. *Splish-splosh*, in they went, the canoe's little feet paddling away, till they came to the place where the fish were thickest.

Hip-hop! Those fish came jumping into the canoe. The prow turned itself round and opened its mouth and—*snip-snap!*—it swallowed the lot.

Those fish were still jumping. So the man gathered up the rest, the canoe took him back to the shore and he carried the fish home for supper.

★   ★   ★

Next day he went fishing again in his magic canoe—
swish-swish! through the bushes; *flip-flop!* along the forest
path. *Splish-splosh!* into the water. *Hip-hop!* the fish came
jumping.

The man started gathering them up—oh, dear!

What had he forgotten?

He'd clean forgotten his manners.

The first catch of fish wasn't his to take.

The prow turned round and glared at him.

It opened its mouth and swallowed the fish—
snip-snap!

Then—*snip-snap!*—it swallowed him too!

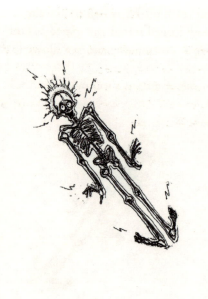

The Butterfly

Last night I dreamed that I was a butterfly.
Now I'm awake again.
At least, I think I am.

But how can I be sure that I'm not a butterfly dreaming of being me?

The Long Road Home

He'd missed the last bus and it was a long walk home. But he'd had a good evening and there was a full moon to light him along the country lanes. He hadn't gone but half a mile out of town when he heard footsteps behind him. He stopped, turned, and saw that the owner of the footsteps had stopped too.

Our lad called out to him, 'Come on, then! Let's walk along together.'

The stranger didn't answer. Didn't move, till our lad set off again and heard footsteps following along behind.

So he stopped again. So did the other fellow.

Our lad called out to him, 'Do I know you?'

No answer.

On they went again, our lad quickening his footsteps now. But each time he glanced back, the other fellow was just that little bit closer.

The first car that came along, he'd flag it down and beg a lift. But there were no cars on the road that night. Just himself and the silent stranger.

He was running when he reached the crossroads. The other fellow was running too. Any minute now he expected to feel hot breath on the back of his neck. And then what?

Then he heard the *clip-clop* of hooves and a pony and trap came trotting round the corner.

'Stop! Please, stop!'

The driver stopped.

'Can you give me a lift, please?'

The driver nodded and our lad climbed up beside him.

Off they went again. No sound now but the *clip-clop* of the pony's hooves. Our lad turned once to look behind and saw only the empty road stretching away in the moonlight. Not a shadow moved in the open fields on either side. He leaned back and smiled to himself.

Here was a tale to tell on winter evenings with the lights turned low!

'Do you believe in ghosts?' he asked.

The driver turned his head towards him and in the cold moonlight he saw that the driver had no face.

And the pony trotted on—*clip-clop*, *clip-clop*—into the dark.

The Enormous Frog

Once upon a time there was a frog the size of a mountain.

Imagine that!

Along came a snake whose tail curled right round the earth.

Imagine that!

The snake whose tail curled round the earth swallowed the frog the size of a mountain.

Along came a crow so huge, its wings covered the whole sky.

Imagine that!

The crow whose wings covered the sky ate the snake whose tail curled round the earth, that swallowed the frog the size of a mountain.

It flew up into the sky and perched on the top of a tree that towered up halfway to the moon.

Imagine that!

Along came a giant who pulled up the tree, on which perched the crow whose wings could cover the sky, who ate the snake whose tail curled round the earth, who swallowed the frog the size of a mountain.

Imagine that!

Then a voice thundered from the heavens above.

38

'That's enough, junior! Playtime's over. Time for bed.'

Imagine that!

Horace

There was Father Bear and Mother Bear, Grandmother Bear, Grandfather Bear, Big Brother Bear, Little Sister Bear, and Horace.

One morning Father Bear went hunting. When he came home that night, Mother Bear, Grandfather Bear, Big Brother, Little Sister, and Horace all came out to meet him.

'Where's Grandmother?' he asked.

'Horace ate her.'

'I was hungry,' said Horace.

'Fair enough,' said Father.

Next day Father Bear went hunting again. When he came home, there were Mother Bear, Big Brother, Little Sister, and Horace, all waiting.

'Where's Grandfather Bear?'

'Horace ate him.'

'I was hungry,' said Horace.

'Fair enough,' said Father.

Next day when he came back from hunting, there were Big Brother, Little Sister, and Horace. No Mother Bear.

'Did Horace eat her?' asked Father.

They nodded.

'Because he was hungry?'

Horace nodded.

'This is getting to be a habit,' said Father.

Next day Father went hunting again and when he came back, there were just Little Sister and Horace.

'Don't tell me,' said Father. 'Horace ate Big Brother. That wasn't very nice.'

'That's right,' said Little Sister.

The next day when Father got back from hunting he found Horace all alone.

'I was hungry,' said Horace.

'Oh, Horace!' said Father Bear. 'What am I going to do with you?'

The next day, Father Bear stayed home to keep an eye on Horace.

The day after that, Horace went hunting.

The Black Velvet Band

She was the prettiest little creature that ever walked on two legs, was Lisa-May. Hair the colour of ripe corn; eyes as blue as the summer sky; and a pretty little turned-up nose that reminded Jake of the puppy he had when he was three years old.

From the evening they first met at the harvest hoedown, it was like Jake's heart-strings were all tangled up with that black velvet band Lisa-May wore round her neck.

Night and day she wore it; summer and winter; springtime and fall. It looked a little strange when they went swimming in the creek together, but whenever Jake mentioned it, Lisa-May would go all coy.

'If we was fiancée'd,' said Jake, 'you wouldn't have no secrets from me.'

'I hope that's not the only reason you're asking me to be your fee-an-say!'

'Darn it! No! I love you, Lisa-May.'

So they got engaged. But she still wouldn't tell him the reason why she wore that black velvet band.

Jake was patient. Come the day when they were man and wife, she'd have to tell him.

So they were married and that night in their

42

honeymoon hotel, Jake said: 'Now I'm your lawful wedded husband, Lisa-May and you're my lawful wedded wife, I'm ordering you to take off that black velvet band!'

So she took the black velvet band from round her neck.

And her head fell off.

Crossroads

'Here's to George!' Tom lifted his pint pot.

'He was a good old boy,' said Dick.

'Why did Death have to take him?' pondered Harry.

'If I knew where Death lived,' said Dick. 'I'd go round his house and I'd ask him that.'

'I'd punch him on the nose!' said Harry.

'I'd do better than that!' said Tom. 'I'd kill Death, stone dead, for what he did to poor old George!'

'If you're looking for Death,' murmured the old man who always sat in the corner by the fire, 'turn left as you go out, keep straight on and you'll meet him at the crossroads.'

'Is that so?'

Off they went, weaving their mazy way towards the crossroads where they found no sign of Death, but only, as they cast about and cast about, a crockful of gold pieces!

'I think,' said Tom, 'another drink is called for!'

'To celebrate?' suggested Dick.

'Egg-sackly!'

Harry—being the youngest and the soberest on a vote of two-to-one—was sent for supplies while the

44

other two stood guard. And while they stood they fell
to considering whether a crock of gold divided between
two fine fellows wouldn't be worth a whole lot more
than the same crock of gold divided between three.

When Harry came back, carrying a jug of the finest
ale, the other two fell on him and made short work of
him.

While they divided up the gold—one for you and
one for me—they downed the jug of ale Harry had
brought. Too late they discovered that his mind had
been running on much the same lines as theirs. A crock
of gold for one would be so much better than a crock
of gold divided between three—or even two. So he'd
popped into the chemist's on the way back, for a little
extra something to add to that ale.

So Tom, Dick, and Harry found Death after all,
waiting for them at the crossroads, just as the old man
in the chimney-corner had promised.

Twice Bitten

A farmer leading a sheep to market turned to look behind him and found he was dragging nothing but a piece of rope behind him through the dust.

There was his prize ewe, disappearing over the crown of the hill! And the thief who'd stolen her scampering after. Too far away for the farmer to do anything about it.

On his way home that evening, who should he meet but that same thief, sitting on the edge of a roadside well.

'You!' said the farmer.

'Me?' said the thief, leaping up. 'Look what you've done now!'

'What I've done? What about what you've done? You stole my prize ewe!'

'Guilty! I admit it.' The thief held up his hands. 'I got a good price for her, too. The money's yours, if you'll promise not to turn me in.'

'Where is it?'

'Ah! That's the problem. When you came up and startled me just now, I dropped it down the well.'

'Oh,' said the farmer.

'Tell you what,' said the thief. 'One of us could lower the other down the well to fetch it.'

'Right,' said the farmer.

'You're the lighter; I'm the stronger. You'd better be the one to go down.'

So the farmer took off his shoes and most of his clothes, so as not to get them wet, and let the thief lower him down to the bottom of the well.

Then the thief dropped the rope in after him and ran off with the farmer's shoes and clothes.

The Man Who Sold His Beard

Poor Jordi!

'I'd give anything to have a beard like yours!' he said to Janos.

'Anything?' Janos's beard was long and thick and silky. Jordi had never managed to grow a beard at all.

'Anything. Well, within reason.'

So they did a deal. Money changed hands.

The beard went on growing on Janos's chin; but now Jordi was the owner. It was his duty—and his pleasure!—to comb it, stroke it, wash it . . .

He started turning up at Janos's house at odd times, just so he could stroke his beard. He trimmed it into interesting shapes. He dyed it blue—then pink—then purple with yellow stripes.

'You can't do that!' said Janos.

'It's my beard,' said Jordi. 'I can do what I like with it.'

'But I have to live with it!' said Janos. 'So does my wife. And must you come climbing in the bedroom window at two in the morning?'

'You were sleeping with it inside the covers,' said Jordi. 'I much prefer it outside. By the way, I've brought this new pomade to spread on my beard. Hold still.' It smelt like horse-dung.

Time and again, Janos tried to sneak round to the barber's so he could have the wretched thing shaved off, but he always seemed to bump into Jordi on the way. Each time they met Jordi would give the beard a tweak and a tug: 'That's a beard to be proud of!'

At last, Janos offered to buy his beard back.

Jordi laughed and shook his head. 'I wouldn't think of it!'

'I'd pay you twice what you paid me!'

'Twice?'

'Three times—four!'

'Done! I was beginning to think it was too much trouble anyway—having to be forever washing and combing and trimming. You're welcome to it back! Four times the price I paid, you said?'

So they did a deal.

Poor Janos!

The Leprechaun

'Oh! The big stone! Oooooh! The big stone's on top of me! OoooooooH! Bejazus, will you let me out from under!'

Paddy stopped in the road and looked about. There, right enough, was a big stone lying by the roadside, with a pair of feet sticking out one end and a wisp of a ginger beard the other.

So he found himself a good stout stick and levered up the stone.

·Out popped a leprechaun. If you think he should have been squashed flat as a pancake, you know nothing at all about leprechauns. He was as right as ninepence. 'I'm grateful to you, Paddy,' he said. 'So grateful, I'm going to grant you three wishes.'

'In that case, I wish,' said Paddy, swaying slightly on his toes, 'I wish I had a pint of stout.'

And there was a bottle of the hard stuff in his hand. He eased the top off and took a sip. It was good stuff, right enough.

'So what's your next wish?' asked the leprechaun. 'Come on, now, I haven't got all night.'

'I wish,' said Paddy, taking another sip, 'that this bottle would never be empty.'

'Done!'

Paddy tested it out; drained the bottle and watched it fill itself to the brim again: magic!

'Come on, come on!' said the leprechaun. 'You've still got wish number three.'

Paddy gazed at the bottle long and hard, gave a hiccup and said, 'Sure, that's no problem. No problem at all. I'll just have another one of these.'

The King of the Cats

A little old woman sat knitting by the fireside, the cat dozing at her feet, when her little old man came in.

Said the little old man to the little old woman: 'As I was taking the short cut home through the churchyard, I saw the strangest thing.'

The old woman put down her knitting. 'What was it you saw?' she asked.

'Do we know anyone called Tom Tilldrum?'

'I don't think so,' she said. 'Go on. You were coming through the churchyard.'

'And I saw nine cats walking towards me, sort of a procession kind of thing.'

The cat pricked up its ears at that.

'The first cat,' said the old man, 'was wearing a plain white collar, like the parson does on Sundays. The next was wearing a top hat with a black ribbon tied round it. After him came six more, walking two by two, pushing a little flat-bed cart between them. And on that cart was a little cat-sized coffin, with a little gold crown balanced on top. Last of all came a pretty little white cat, wearing a black veil on her head.'

'That would be the widow, I suppose. A cat funeral! Well, well! Do you hear that, old Tom?'

The cat heard it. He was sitting up and washing himself, the way cats do, pretending to be quite unconcerned.

'So anyway,' the little old man went on, 'I took off my hat to show proper respect and stood back to let them go past. But they stopped right beside me. And the one in the top-hat turned and spoke! He said, "Would you kindly tell Tom Tilldrum that Tim Tilldrum's dead?" But I'm blessed if I know who Tom Tilldrum is or where I'm supposed to find him!'

'Tom knows!' she cried.

The cat was fairly dancing round the room, chasing its own tail and leaping over the furniture. 'Tim Tilldrum's dead!' it cried. 'Tim Tilldrum's dead! So now I'm the King of the Cats!' It stood up on its hind legs, whirled round and round until it was no more than a blur, then took off like a rocket, straight up the chimney.

And was never seen again.

Old Ted (5)

'I remember,' said Old Ted, 'as if it were yesterday. I remember when I was a lad. I remember the day Squire bought himself a new horse—beautiful! a thoroughbred. The only trouble was, no one could ride him. He threw them all off—the Squire and his sons and the grooms and the stable lads; one after another they all bit the dust.

'I was just the gardener's boy, but "Let me try!" I said. "Take off that saddle."

'So they took off the saddle.

'"Now hold him steady," I said.

'So they held him steady.

'I walked up to that beautiful, thoroughbred horse and I looked him in the eye.

'I breathed slow and steady into his nostrils.

'I whispered the horseman's word that was taught me by an old gypsy horse-coper.

'Then I leapt up on his back—and do you know what?'

'What?'

'Darn me, but I couldn't stay on him either!'

Old Ted (6)

Old Ted put up a sign on the barn: 'Fifty p to see the horse with a tail where its head should be!'

That ought to be a sight for sore eyes! I watched the people going in. They didn't stay long. Out they came again, shaking their heads and frowning at Ted.

A horse with a tail where its head ought to be! Shocking!

Only a few of the younger ones shook their heads like the rest, glanced at the queue standing waiting, and grinned at one another.

That wasn't nice.

A horse with a tail where its head ought to be! That's nothing to laugh at.

But I had to see for myself.

I paid my fifty p and I stepped inside. There stood the horse, tethered back-to-front, poor thing, with its tail hanging over the manger, where its head ought to be.

More fool me!

Something for a Rainy Day

An old man lay dying. He didn't feel too bad about it. He'd had a good life; made a little money; married a lovely wife who'd given him two fine sons, both doing well.

To make sure there'd be no arguments about it after he was gone, he divided his fortune straight down the middle, half to each son.

'Nothing for your wife?' the lawyer asked.

'My sons are good sons! They'll look after their mother.'

But the first son treated his widowed mother like an unpaid servant; cooking and cleaning and minding the children. At the other son's house she was tucked away in a wee small room and forgotten about entirely.

So back and forth she went between one son and the other, till she happened to meet an old friend from her schooldays: 'How lovely to see you!' said her friend. 'But how pale you look! Still grieving for your husband? He was a good man. And your sons and your grandchildren—how are they?'

The poor widow burst into tears. What could her old friend do but take her home? After she'd heard the whole sad story, 'You'd be welcome to stay here,' she said. 'But your sons should be ashamed of themselves and your grandchildren should learn the proper way to treat their grandmother.' She handed her two leather bags.

'What's this?' One was all lumpy; the other sagged as if it was filled with dust.

'Just a little something for a rainy day. No! Don't look inside. My guess is you'll never need to.'

No more she did. When the two sons saw those two heavy bags—what was in them? Gold dust? Diamonds?—everything changed. They tumbled over one another to please her. The old lady lived in comfort for the rest of her days, watching her grandchildren grow.

She left those two leather bags she'd been keeping for a rainy day to her two loving sons. With trembling fingers they opened them up. And found one filled with stones, the other with dust.

The Cow That Ate the Piper

Here's a poor piper, travelling the roads of old Ireland. Times are hard; the weather's freezing and him with no shoes to his feet. So when he came upon a dead man lying by the road and his feet frozen stiff inside his fine new boots, it seemed the most natural thing in the world to hack the feet off, boots and all, thinking to thaw them off later.

So on went the piper and fell in with three other fellers. And on they went again till they came to a farmhouse and begged a meal and a place to sleep that cold night.

The meal wasn't bad, but it was a poor sort of place, one room down and one up, and a cow looking over the low stone wall between the living room and the byre.

'Keep well away from that cow,' said the farmer's wife, 'or she'll eat the hair off your head and the clothes off your back while you're sleeping.'

Then the farmer and his wife went up the ladder to their bed and the four travellers lay down to sleep. But not before the piper had taken his fine new boots out of his bag and set them by the fire to thaw.

In the morning the farmer's wife came down to make

58

breakfast. There where they'd left four men sleeping now lay but three! Nothing left of the other but a pair of feet and the cow with a satisfied smile on her face.

She ran back upstairs and woke her husband: 'The cow!' she said. 'The cow has eaten the piper!' She took him downstairs and showed him the evidence.

The farmer made haste to wake the three sleepers. 'Sorry!' he said. 'Sorry! Sorry! There'll be no breakfast for you this morning. There's sickness in the house. You'd best be on your way.' He pressed a golden guinea into each man's hand as he ushered them out of the door. 'Not a word of this, mind! Please call again.'

Off they went, very surprised to find themselves on the road so early in the morning. More surprised still to hear music playing somewhere up ahead—and to find the piper dancing to his own music, capering in his fine, new boots!

The Big Stone

I asked about and asked about, but nobody knew how long the big stone had lain there, slap-bang in the middle of the village green.

One day I climbed up on top of it and started picking away at the moss that grew there. I found some letters carved. So I picked away a bit more until I could spell out the words:

PLEASE TURN ME OVER

Everyone agreed the words could only mean one thing. There was something hidden underneath that stone. Treasure, maybe? What else?

All the village turned out to help turn that big stone over. They came armed with crowbars and sticks and good old-fashioned elbow-grease. We pushed and we shoved. We huffed and we puffed. We put wedges underneath, so the big stone wouldn't roll back and hurt someone while we were turning it. Then we pushed and shoved some more.

Together we turned that big stone over. It settled down on its other side with something that sounded like a sigh.

There was nothing underneath but a muddy hole. I climbed up on top and brushed the mud away and found more words carved.

THIS SIDE UP
THANK YOU

Chien Yang

First they were children together; then they were sweethearts; and they thought it would not be long till they were happy-ever-aftering together.

But Chien Yang's father had other ideas. He was a rich man and Wang Chou was just a poor clerk. Wang Chou was sent away to the big city.

Chien Yang thought her heart would break. She lay down on her bed and would not eat or speak or sleep.

Though Wang Chou was far away, it seemed as if Chien Yang was with him still, in the sunlight on still water; in the sighing of the wind; in the scent of orange blossom wafted on the night breeze.

Out of the moonlight and shadows she came walking. 'I could not let you go,' she said.

Together they lived for five years in the city. They were not rich, but they were not poor. And they were happy, except for one thing. In all that time, they heard not one word from Chien Yang's father. 'I must go back to see him,' she said.

So back they went.

'I am afraid,' she said. 'Afraid of my father's anger.'

So Wang Chou walked up alone to the house, leaving her by the roadside. And was greeted by her father like a long-lost son! 'If only I had let you marry her!' he said. 'Poor Chien Yang!'

'Poor Chien Yang?'

'She has not eaten or spoken or slept since the day you left!'

'Chien Yang is well and happy. I left her just now, by the roadside!'

Each one thought the other was stark, staring mad.

'I'll fetch her. You'll see for yourself.'

'I'll fetch her.' Wang Chou hurried back down the hill, while Chien Yang's father went to her room and found his daughter up and dressed.

Up the hill came Chien Yang, tired of waiting.

Down the hill Chien Yang ran to meet her, the two more like one another than two mirror images, so no one could tell which was which, falling into each other's arms, laughing, hand to hand, mouth to mouth, long hair twining.

And then there was one.

Pig!

He was Jack-the-Lad in his brand-new company car.

Nought-to-sixty in however-many seconds! Stereo turned up full volume.

Oh, yes! he was Somebody now, he thought, tossing his empty Coke-can out of the window.

'Pig!' yelled the driver coming the other way, having to pull hard over to avoid him.

'Pig yourself!' he yelled back, leaning out of the window as he turned the corner.

Too late he saw the pig, standing in the middle of the road.

Double Trouble

He was a poor man, and never going to be any richer, no matter how long he lived. To keep body and soul together when times were hard, he'd borrowed from the money-lender; borrowed more than he could ever repay. And the interest kept mounting up, till for every rupee he earned to keep himself and his family, he had to pay two rupees to the money-lender.

He prayed to the god Vishnu: 'Lord, I know this is my fate in this life and I do try to bear it patiently. But could you give me just a little help? For the sake of my wife and my poor children.'

Vishnu heard his prayer and granted the poor man three wishes.

But even then the money-lender still got double.

The poor man wished for a bag of gold—and next thing he heard, the money-lender was crowing about finding himself suddenly richer by two bags of gold!

The poor man wished for a well of fresh water—and lo! the money-lender began selling the sweet water from his second well at a handsome profit.

So, for his third wish, the poor man wished to be struck blind in one eye.

The Yellow Gloves

Never go down to the end of town. Don't ever knock at the door of the big white house. Nor speak to the little old man that lives there.

That's what Molly's mother told her. Molly never would have disobeyed if she hadn't lost her new yellow gloves. She looked for them everywhere else, but she didn't find them. So down to the end of town she went and knocked at the door of the big white house.

The little old man opened it. He was old and he was ugly and he was vile. 'Have you come for your new yellow gloves, Molly?' he said. 'Take them—but if you tell anyone where you found them, I'll have you for sure!'

So Molly went home and when her mother asked her where she found them, Molly said: 'I can't tell you that. If I do the little old man in the big white house says he'll have me for sure!'

Then her mother locked the door and barred the windows, and stoked the fire so the little old man from the big white house couldn't come down the chimney. But as Molly lay in bed that night and the clock began striking twelve—BOM!—she heard the creak of the bottom stair.

She heard the old man's voice whisper: 'Molly, I'm coming for you. Molly, I'm up one step!'

BOM! 'Molly, I'm up two steps!'

BOM! 'Molly, I'm up three steps!'

BOM! 'Molly, I'm up four steps!'

BOM! 'Molly, I'm up five steps!'

BOM! 'Molly, I'm up six steps!'

BOM! 'Molly, I'm up seven steps!'

BOM! 'Molly, I'm up eight steps!'

BOM! 'Molly, I'm up nine steps!'

BOM! 'Molly, I'm up ten steps!'

BOM! 'Molly, I'm up eleven steps!'

BOM! 'Molly, I'm up at the top of the stairs.'

'Molly, I HAVE YOU NOW!'

Timber!

His name was Erysichthon—Eric for short. He was a woodcutter. There's no end to the things you can do with a nice bit of wood. Build a house, or a boat; make a chair or a table; build a fire to cook your food and keep you warm in winter.

All good things must come to an end. Soon the people for miles around had more wood than they knew what to do with.

But Eric had the bit between his teeth now; cutting wood was what he was best at, so he went on cutting down trees, storing it against the day when folks needed wood again, till there wasn't a tree left for miles around. Only the grove sacred to the goddess Ceres, who loves all growing things; the flowers, the fruit, and the harvest corn. And trees. Ceres was especially fond of trees.

'Daddy, please—no!' begged his daughter, Mestra.

Eric pushed her aside, rolled up his sleeves, picked up his axe, and set to work.

Mestra prayed to the goddess: 'Please don't be too hard on him! He never used to be like this. It's like a fever—a hunger—'

'Hunger!' roared Ceres. 'I'll teach him what hunger is!'

Eric put down his axe. 'Time for a little snack,' he

said, and set off home to see what there was to eat. Some cheese would be nice—with a few olives—and a loaf or two of bread and—

By the time Mestra got home, the larder was empty.

'What's for dinner?' demanded Eric. 'I'm hungry!'

Off went Mestra, to the market.

Came back and found he'd boiled his boots and eaten them. He was just finishing off the laces. 'Ah, meat!' he cried. 'Don't bother to cook it. I'll eat it raw.'

Day after day, Eric just kept on eating.

Mestra spent every penny they'd saved on food to keep her father going. For a while she was having the food delivered by the cartload. Till one day the carter came out and found one of his oxen missing and Eric eyeing the other with malice aforethought.

The money ran out, but he was still hungry. If there was no food on the table, he'd nibble at the wooden plates and cups, till they were all gone too. And after that the tablecloth, the curtains, and the rugs . . .

'Feed me!' he moaned, nibbling at his fingernails, till they were worn down to his fingers' ends. 'Feed me!' He bit off a finger and started munching it, crunching the bones between his teeth. 'Mm! Nice.' He bit off another. 'I wonder if toes taste the same. Mm-mm! Cheese and onion. My favourite.'

Mestra ran down to the marketplace: 'Help me! Help me! My father's so hungry, he's eating his own fingers and toes!'

For a while no one believed her. Then they decided to go and see for themselves. By that time, it was too late. All that was left of Eric was his head, lying on the floor.

'Feed me!' it said.

Cat and Mouse

A cat and a mouse set up house together. Yes they did!

They managed things very well to begin with. They saved up their pennies and bought a pot of dripping to keep them through the lean winter months. And, so they wouldn't be tempted to touch it before the hard times came, they took it down to the church and hid it in the vestry.

Oh, the smell of that dripping! The cat wished it was winter already. She began to dream of dripping, even when she was awake. At last she said to the mouse: 'I'm off to the church today. My sister's baby's being christened.'

There was no christening. Cat went straight to the pot of dripping and creamed off the top. Oh, the taste of that dripping!

'How did the christening go?' asked the mouse, when the cat got home. 'What's the baby's name?'

Cat thought fast: 'Top-off!' she said.

'Top-off!' said Mouse. 'That's an odd name.'

It wasn't long before Cat was off to the church again—this time, for her other sister's wedding.

There was no wedding; only a pot of delicious

70

dripping that was half-gone by the time Cat came home, still cleaning her whiskers.

'Half-gone?' said the mouse. 'Is that your sister's married name? That's a very odd name, to be sure.'

But she was a trusting soul. She even trusted Cat when she said she must be off to the church again. This time, she said it was for her grandmother's funeral. And when Mouse asked her what was her grandmother's name? Why, Granny Cleangone, Cat told her, without so much as a blush.

Time went by and winter came and Cat kept saying times weren't that hard; no need to dip into their store of dripping yet. Till the mouse went on her own to fetch it back. And found the jar licked clean.

Then she began putting two and two together: Top-off? Half-gone? Cleangone? 'You!' she cried. 'It was you!'

Cat drew herself up indignantly: 'What do you mean? Some thief has stolen our dripping and—'

'It was you!' Mouse bounced up and down with rage. 'Top-off! I thought that was an odd name.'

'I'm warning you!' said Cat.

'Half-gone!' squeaked Mouse. 'That was even odder.'

'Not another word!'

'As for all that stuff and nonsense about your grandmother's funeral—what was her name?'

Cat pounced, bit, chewed, and swallowed. 'Cleangone,' she said.

The Wide-Mouth Toad-Frog

The wide-mouth toad-frog left his pond and went hippety-hopping through the big, wide world to see what he could see.

On the farmhouse steps he saw a black, fluffy thing, like a cushion.

'WHO ARE YOU?' yelled the wide-mouth toad-frog. 'WHAT DO YOU EAT?'

The black, fluffy thing uncurled itself, stretched, and yawned. 'I am a cat,' it said. 'I like to eat mice—when I can get them.'

'INTERESTING! I'M A WIDE-MOUTH TOAD-FROG! I'M OFF TO SEE THE WORLD. GOODBYE!'

Off he went, hippety-hop. In the farmyard he saw a fat, pink, oinky thing with a curly tail.

'WHO ARE YOU?' yelled the wide-mouth toad-frog. 'WHAT DO YOU EAT?'

The fat, pink, curly-tailed thing was too busy rootling through the rubbish to look up. 'I am a pig,' it snuffled. 'I like to eat potato peelings and apples and acorns.'

'EXCELLENT! I'M A WIDE-MOUTH TOAD-FROG! I'M OFF TO SEE THE WORLD. GOODBYE!'

Hippety-hop, he came to the meadow. There he saw a big black-and-white creature with sticky-out bits on its head.

'WHO ARE YOU?' yelled the wide-mouth toad-frog. 'WHAT DO YOU EAT?'

The black-and-white creature looked up, but went on chewing. 'I am a cow,' it said. 'I eat mostly grass.'

'AMAZING! I'M A WIDE-MOUTH TOAD-FROG! I'M OFF TO SEE THE WORLD. GOODBYE!'

Off he went again, hippety-hop. In the woods he met a big, brown, furry thing, like a rug.

'WHO ARE YOU?' yelled the wide-mouth toad-frog. 'WHAT DO YOU EAT?'

The big, brown, furry thing stood up on its hind legs and it was huge. 'I am a bear,' it said. 'Honey's what I love to eat best of all.'

'BRILLIANT! I'M A WIDE-MOUTH TOAD-FROG. I'M OFF TO SEE THE WORLD. GOODBYE!'

Hippety-hopping, he came to a river. There on the bank lay a long, green thing, like a log.

'WHO ARE YOU? WHAT DO YOU EAT?'

The green, loggy thing opened its jaws and smiled, showing two rows of sharp, pointy teeth. 'I am an alligator,' it said. 'I just love to eat wide-mouth toad-frogs. Have you seen any round here, by any chance?'

The wide-mouth toad-frog pursed up his mouth very small and said in a teeny-tiny voice: 'Wide-mouth toad-frogs? No, no! I don't think I ever saw one of those, never in all my travels through the big, wide world!'

Dream Lover

She was a chief's daughter, and beautiful as the morning sun. She could have had any man she chose.

Instead she dreamed herself a dream lover, beautiful as the moon. Black his hair as the crow-bird's wing; eyes the blue of turquoise; his lips tasting of honey.

Night after night she dreamed him, till on the night of the full moon he came for her: 'Come with me!' he whispered. 'Quickly. Come! Come!'

So she left her father's lodge and followed her dream lover, across the sleeping plain. In beauty they walked until the sun rose and they lay down to sleep.

Night came and on they went again. Softly he walked, leaving no footprints in the dewy grass. Sweet his voice, like the sighing of the summer wind.

Night after night she followed him across the whispering plain, through the echoing forest and up, up into the high, bare mountains.

Till one evening at the dark of the moon she woke to find nothing but a handful of crow's feathers scattered beside her; and two turquoise stones; and the taste of honey on her mouth.

She was alone on the cold mountainside.

Contrary Mary

I f he said chalk, she said cheese. He'd say black and she'd say white. If he thought it was going to be a fine day, she'd go straight back indoors to fetch her umbrella.

How Sam had put up with Contrary Mary all these years was a mystery.

'It's being contrary that keeps her cheerful,' he said. 'Isn't it, Mary?'

'No, it's not!' she said.

'There!' said Sam. 'You see?'

Thirty years they'd been together—

'Twenty-nine!' said Mary.

'—thirty, come tatty-hoiking time,' Sam went on, as if there'd been no interruption. 'It was at Easter we first started walking out together.'

'May! It wasn't Easter; it was May!'

'May or Easter, we used to walk along by the river, just as we're doing now. You wore the prettiest little straw bonnet. It had blue ribbons.'

'Green! The ribbons were green!'

'Aye, I remember we had this same argument even

then. I said blue; you said green. And I got so mad, I took my knife—'

'—my scissors!'

'My knife, I said; and cut 'em off!'

'With my scissors!'

'It was my knife I used.'

'Scissors!' Contrary Mary was so busy arguing, she lost her footing and fell head-first into the river. 'Scissors!' she cried as she came up for air.

'Knife! Say knife and I'll help you out.'

'Scissors! Scissors! Scissors!' she screamed as the water covered her head once—twice—three times. Then the river carried her away.

All the next day they searched for her body, but there was no sign.

'There's no sign of her,' they told poor Sam.

'Where were you looking?' he asked.

'Downstream, of course; the way the river would have taken her.'

Sam shook his head: 'She was always contrary. Try looking upstream.'

Sure enough, upstream's where they found her, with the two fingers of her right hand sticking upright—just like a pair of scissors!

The Scorpion and the Frog

A frog sat sunning himself on a lily pad in the cool morning mist. Later the sun would grow too hot. He'd have to crawl away and find himself a patch of shade. But for the moment life was good. Life was just perfect.

'Mr Frog! Mr Frog? Excuse me, Mr Frog!'

Frog turned his head, to see a scorpion scuttling backwards and forwards on the riverbank.

'What is it?' he asked.

'Mr Frog, I hardly like to ask—but I wonder if you would be so kind as to carry me to the other side of the river.'

'No way!' said Frog. He'd been warned about scorpions when he was scarcely more than a tadpole. Scorpions had a sting that would kill you stone dead in under a minute.

'Please, Mr Frog! My sister's sick and there's no one to look after her seven children.'

'No,' said Frog, just a bit miffed at having his fine morning spoiled.

'Please!' begged the scorpion. 'For the sake of my sister's soon-to-be-motherless children. Are you afraid I might sting you? That would be stupid, wouldn't it? You'd sink—and I'd be drowned.'

It was a nice morning, after all. It gave you the sort of good feeling you wanted to share. So Frog hopped over to the bank and let the scorpion climb onto his back.

He hadn't swum but halfway across the river when he felt the deadly sting of the scorpion's tail.

'What did you do that for?' he cried. 'Now we're both done for!'

'I'm a scorpion,' shrugged the scorpion. 'It's what scorpions do.'

Old Ted (7)

'This Egyptian mummy,' said the guide, 'is two thousand five hundred years old.'

'I make it two thousand five hundred and three,' said Ted.

The guide looked at him a bit surprised, but she pressed on.

'This Roman vase,' she said, 'is one thousand eight hundred years old.'

'Shouldn't that be one thousand eight hundred and three?' asked Ted.

The guide gave him a nasty look.

'This Viking sword,' she said, 'is twelve hundred years old.'

'I think,' said Ted, 'you'll find it's twelve hundred and three.'

'Shush!' I told him. 'You'll get us thrown out. What do you know anyway about archaeology?'

'I was here three years ago,' said Ted. 'She's telling us the same now as she did then. I don't know much about archaeology, but I can do simple arithmetic.'

Old Ted (8)

'Poor old Uncle Charlie!' Ted shook his head. 'He's been gone a long time.'

'Gone, Ted? Packed his bags and left, sort of thing?'

Ted shook his head. 'Oh! You mean Gone, as in dead?'

'Ah!' said Ted. 'You tell me. Poor old Uncle Charlie. It was his hobby was his downfall.'

'What hobby was that, Old Ted?'

'Holes. Some people like football; others go bird-watching; Uncle Charlie was into digging holes. One day he dug a hole that perfect, he decided to take it home, to show his wife.

'So he fetched his old truck and dug up the hole; loaded it on the back and set off.

'He hadn't gone no more than half a mile when he drove over a bump. Felt a jolt; looked back; saw the hole lying in the road behind him.

'No damage done, not that he could see. Hole still as good as new.

'So Charlie starts reversing back towards it. That hole's no lightweight. The closer he gets, the easier it's going to be to load it up again.

'Gently does it—just a bit further—back, back, back—easy now! Too late.

'At the very last moment, his foot slipped from the brake to the accelerator.

'Down the hole went Charlie, truck and all. And hasn't been seen from that day to this. Poor old Uncle Charlie! He's been gone a long time.'

Bearskin

Times were hard. Times were pretty-nigh
desperate. Chas and Jake thought up a way to
keep the wolf from the door, so to speak.
Though it wasn't wolves that were on their minds, but
bears. One bear would do.

'If we could kill a bear—' said Jake.

'And sell its skin?' Chas was ahead of him.

'Reckon we could live off that until the spring
comes!'

'Reckon we could at that!'

So off they went and did a deal with the fur trader.
Got enough in advance to keep them in supplies while
they went hunting bears.

Till they found one.

That bear was huge! And he was mean! (So would
you be, at having your winter sleep disturbed by a
couple of no-good has-beens!)

Jake took one look and headed up the nearest tree.
Which was a pretty dumb thing to do, since a bear can
climb a tree faster and better than a man.

So it was lucky for him Chas tripped over his own
two feet and fell face down in the snow and lay too
scared out of his own skin to move a muscle.

The bear moseyed up to him and sniffed him up and down.

Chas didn't move.

Must be dead! thought the bear. Sniffed again, to make certain-sure, paying particular attention to his head.

Chas held his breath.

He's dead! the bear decided. Bears don't care for dead meat. Dead meat's like finishing off the leftovers from someone else's plate. If you're a bear.

So the bear went lumbering on his way. Jake climbed down out of his tree. Chas sat up.

'Boy oh boy!' Jake shook his head. 'When that old bear put his head down close to yours, I thought you were a goner for sure.'

Chas was still shaking. 'Oh, that! He was just whispering a word of advice. He said in future we should maybe kill the bear first—then sell its skin!'

Old Ted (9)

'That's a most remarkable Old English sheepdog you've got lying outside your door,' said the stranger. 'And a pint of your very best ale, landlord, if you please.'

'Remarkable, is he?' said the landlord, drawing off a pint of bitter, the same as the rest were drinking.

'Amazing!'

'How so?'

'As I came in, he spoke to me!'

'Old Monty? Never!'

'He lifted up his head and said "Good morning", as sure as I'm standing here drinking your most excellent ale.'

The landlord shook his head: 'Thick as two planks is Old Monty. Old Monty's never said a word in his life.'

'It must have been the dog,' the stranger insisted. 'I looked all round and there was no one about. No one at all.'

'Ah! But was there another dog with him?' asked Old Ted, from his seat by the window.

'Another dog?' The stranger thought carefully. 'Now you come to mention it, yes, there was. A scruffy sort of mongrel.'

'Ah!' said Ted. 'That explains it. That one's my dog. He's a ventriloquist.'

Who's a Donkey?

There was a student of Salamanca, making his way back to college after a good weekend. His head ached. His feet ached. What wouldn't he give for a ride on that donkey, tethered there, outside a peasant's cottage! But his pockets were empty and he didn't think the peasant would lend him the donkey for nothing. So our student hatched a cunning plan.

When the peasant came out of his hovel, there was no sign of the donkey; only the student kneeling there, wearing the donkey's bridle.

'Who are you?' asked the peasant.

The student looked down at himself, at his hands and feet and all the rest between. 'Was I dreaming?' he asked. 'Or did it really happen? I dreamed that I was a donkey. Wait a minute! I remember my professor—who is also some kind of a magician, so they say—I remember him telling me I wasn't studying hard enough. If I was so set on being a donkey, he said . . . And then—and then—Oh! Could he have turned me into a donkey? What do you think?'

The poor man didn't know what to think. There was only the evidence of his own two eyes to go on.

'Well, you've been a good worker for me,' he said, taking off the bridle.

'I'll tell my professor you said so. What is your name, by the way?'

'Antonio.'

'Antonio. I'll remember. Goodbye.'

The student collected Antonio's donkey from round the corner, where he'd hidden it, and rode the rest of the way back to Salamanca.

Later in the day, Antonio was walking into town to buy himself a new donkey, when he came upon his old donkey tethered to a tree. Round its neck hung a notice: 'Please take me back to Antonio the peasant.'

Antonio shook his head: 'Upset your professor again, have you? Come on, then, let's go home. I wonder how many years you'll be working for me this time.'

Finders Keepers

They were never wreckers. To lure a ship onto the rocks, kill the crew, and make off with the cargo—that was sinful. That was wrong!

They'd never had any truck with wrecking. But if a ship just happened to fetch up on the rocks below the village, well, that was by the will of God and, as to the cargo, it was a case of finders keepers.

When word came during Sunday morning service that there was a ship run aground, they dropped their hymn-books and made for the church door.

'Stop!' cried the vicar in a voice of thunder. 'Bar the door!'

Everyone stopped. The churchwardens made haste to do as they were bid.

The rest stood looking suitably ashamed of themselves, while the vicar tore off his cassock and elbowed his way through to the front of the crowd still clustering round the door.

'Right!' he said. 'Now we'll all start fair. Unbar the door!'

The Way to Heaven

He'd lived a hard life, but a good one, 'And you'll get your reward in heaven,' the priest told him.

'Will I, though?' the old man said.

'You have my word on it.'

'What do you know? You're just guessing! If I'm not going to heaven, I'm going to have a bit of fun while I'm still down on earth.'

'How can any of us know for sure if we're going to heaven?' the priest sighed.

'We can go up there and ask!' said the old man. That's what he decided to do. He took the biggest step-ladder he could find and set it up.

His wife sighed. 'Silly old man!' Of course the step-ladder was nowhere near long enough to reach up to heaven.

So he hauled the kitchen table into the yard and set the step-ladder on top of it. Still nowhere near.

Then he started piling up the chairs and the bedstead and the chest-of-drawers.

'You silly old man!' said his wife. 'You'll never get anywhere near heaven.'

'Hold your tongue, woman. Go and ask the neighbours if we can borrow their furniture.'

So she did and the neighbours came, bringing every stick of furniture that wasn't nailed down to add to the pile that was supposed to lead all the way up to heaven. They wanted to see how far he'd get.

'I'm getting there!' he cried. 'I'm getting there!' With the tips of his fingers he could just touch the edge of the lowest cloud. 'I just need one thing more!'

'There's nothing left, you silly old man!' his wife shouted back.

'You silly old woman! Just pull out the kitchen table from the bottom of the pile and pass it up to me.'

'Silly old woman, am I?'

She pulled out the kitchen table from the bottom of the pile, just as he'd told her to do.

Odin

The hall was decked with boughs of holly, mistletoe, and ivy. The Yule log burning brightly on the hearth. 'I see you still keep to the old ways,' the tall stranger said, standing in the doorway.

'The old ways? No!'

'Oh, no! We're all Christians here.'

But it was Christmas Eve after all; the time for goodwill to all men. And outside was bitter cold. So they invited the tall stranger in. Some of them wondered why he never took off his broad-brimmed hat. A few of them noticed the reason; it was to hide the fact that he was blind in one eye. Some of them said afterwards that he was an old man and close to death. Yet he moved with a young man's grace and confidence as he took the place kept by the fire for the unexpected guest. He sat warming his hands on the cup of mulled ale that was offered him.

His voice, when he began to speak, was old and young together, with a strange music in it that stirred forgotten dreams of Thor the Thunderer and Loki the Trickster; of Freya the Beautiful and Odin, who plucked out one of his own eyes and thought it a cheap price to pay for the gift of knowledge of all that is and was and shall be. To while away the hours till midnight, he told them stories of the Old Ones.

'But the old gods are dead!' said the priest.

'Aye,' said the stranger. 'Dead and gone. Gone to a better place, where there is youth without ageing and joy without sorrow. Where blossoms and ripe fruit hang together on the bough. By day they ride and hunt and fight—but if any man falls, he rises again, to feast when night falls in Valhalla! Which, I think, must be a place very much like this—a roaring fire and food fit for a king; music and friendship and tales to tell.'

'But the old gods—the old beliefs—are dead,' the priest said again.

'Aye,' said the stranger. 'All but one.' He took a stub of candle from his pocket, set it on the table beside him and lit it. 'When Odin was born, the three Fates came to foretell his destiny. The first two promised him happiness and victory in battle. The third—worm-tongued—said Odin would live no longer than the candle that burned beside his cradle. At which, his father snuffed the candle out and hid it away, so Odin would live for ever.'

Then the bell rang for the midnight service and they all went off to the cold little church on the hill to welcome the new-born god into the world, leaving the tall, one-eyed stranger still staring into the candle-flame. Dreaming, perhaps, of the old gods and Valhalla.

When they came back, they found the candle burnt out; nothing but a puddle of wax. And the tall stranger lying dead beside it.